I0538136

Copyright © 2014 by Stefan Ellery

All rights reserved. This book or any portion thereof may not be reproduced or used in any manner whatsoever without the express written permission of the publisher except for the use of brief quotations in a book review.

First Printing, 2014
ISBN 978-0-9939890-0-1
www.stefanellery.com

The Meeting of Kalle Rabbit and Pelle Fox

Illustrated and written
by
Stefan Ellery

Acknowledgements

This is for my Morfar who created these two characters to tell made up bedtime stories to my Mother and Aunt. It is also for my Mom who brought Kalle and Pelle to my attention and to the children in my family who I hope will enjoy reading these tales and share them with their families in the future.

Kalle Rabbit was enjoying some juicy cloud berries, when he heard a loud yap and a squeal followed by a sad mewl.

He tried to keep on eating, but the mewling got louder and louder and interrupted the joy he was having eating his juicy snack.

Kalle left the cloud berries and followed the noise. It did not take him very long because the closer he got the louder the mewling became.

Eventually Kalle came upon a clearing with an old well in the middle of it.

The noise became much louder and it hurt his sensitive ears. Kalle not seeing anyone in the field could only assume that the noise came from the well. With his paws covering his ears he aproached the well and looked down.

The well was too dark for him to see the bottom and to see who was making such a racket. Annoyed that he had been unable to eat the cloud berries he yelled at the well.

"Oh please cut that horrible noise out, I can barely think!"

Not expecting a response and feeling satisfied for letting his frustration out Kalle began to leave, but before he could take a single hop a voice called out from the well.

"Oh someone is there, oh very good, very good. I am so glad you heard me."

Kalle still a little frustrated spoke in an irritated voice. "How could I not with the racket you made, humph it is a wonder that I am the only one that showed up. Then again your mewling and yapping may have driven off anyone away with fright."

"Yes, yes, I understand your frustration but please understand mine. I am stuck at the bottom of this well. It is a little damp and the stench is making me gasp. Please, please, get me out."

Kalle much calmer and feeling pity for the one stuck in the well decided he would do what he can to help. "Very well, but do tell me. How did you manage to end up at the bottom of this well?"

"It is a little embarrassing and I would rather not say, but I will tell you once you have helped me out."

"Do you have a name I can call you."

"Yes, yes, I do please call me Pelle."

"Pelle you can call me Kalle." Kalle looked at the well and could not see anything that could help. The bucket hanging above was broken apart and the left over rope was rotten with age.

He looked about the clearing but most of it was bare. He did spy a clump of weeds at the edge of the forest and that gave him an idea. "Pelle I think I have an idea but it shall take a while."

"Yes, yes, but please hurry. The damp is making my bones ache and the smell is making my nose twitch."

"I Shall." Kalle Rabbit ran into the patch of weeds and found what he was looking for. There was a large patch of nettles that he quickly uprooted.

He then stripped the nettles into fibers and began to braid them into a cord. After a lengthy time Kalle Rabbit managed to assemble a cord that was long enough to reach to the bottom of the well.

Kalle returned to the well and called out to Pelle. There was no answer. He called out a little louder and still no answer came.

Kalle Rabbit leaned over the well to make is voice heard more easily. In the process Kalle Rabbit knocked over a small rock. The rock fell into the well. When the rock landed he heard a surprised yelp.

"**O**uch, what, what was that!" Pelle shouted.

"Sorry about that I accidentally knocked a rock into the well while I was trying to get your attention. What are you doing down there anyway. You did not answer any of my calls."

"Well, well, you took such a long time that I became tired and bored and then fell asleep."

"Then it is a good thing that I woke you. I have a long cord to help you out of your predicament."

"Very, very good news indeed."

Kalle looked around the well and found a metal ring sticking out of the ground. He attached the cord and dropped it down the well.

Now Pelle you are going to have to use the rope to climb out. I am not sure I am strong enough to pull you out. Unless of course you are a vole. "

"No, no, not a vole."

"A ferret?"

"Not at all, not at all."

When Kalle saw the rope go taught he knew Pelle was using it to climb out of the well. "How about a skunk?"

"Now, now, I am certainly not a skunk."

Kalle was about say another animals name when Pelle's head stuck out from the well.

"A fox!" Kalle screamed. Kalle rabbit quickly ran away from Pelle and disappeared into the woods.

"Yes, Yes, a Fox. Very good."

Unfortunately for Pelle Fox Kalle was nowhere to be seen. He wanted to thank Kalle for his help getting him out of that nasty well. Pelle was happy to be out of the well and he could feel the ache from his bones fading and he could finally breathe not having to deal with the stench from the well.

Off in the distance he heard a cry and a whimper. It sounded like it came from Kalle he thought to himself.

Pelle rushed off in the direction of the noise and shortly found a rabbit tangled up in the roots of a tree.

Kalle running so fast did not pay attention to his surroundings and ran into a bunch of roots that managed to trap him as good as a hunter's noose. Seeing Pelle approach him he began to beg for his life. "Oh please do not eat me as you can see I am not much of a meal."

Pelle smiled at Kalle and began to pull on the roots. "Now, now, why would I eat the one who saved me from that well besides rabbit is not to my liking. You can stay there if you like or get out. I have loosened the roots so you should be able to get free."

Kalle pulled himself free from the roots and being very curious and thankful remained to talk to Kalle the fox. "Thank you for your help. If you did not free me I would have been someone's meal.

Pelle grinned "That may be, but not by me."

"Ah yes, I believe you were going to tell me how you came about to be in that well."

"True, true, I had been told that if one made a wish at a well that wish would come true. When I found this well I leaned over the wall to make the wish and somehow leaned just a little too far and I fell in."

"Oh my, what was the wish that you had made?"

"Well, well, I wished to have a friend but I think that wish may have been wasted."

Kalle thought to himself and smiled. He held out his paw to Pelle and said. "Hmm I think your wish came true. That is if you would like a rabbit for a friend.

A happy Pelle took Kalle's paw and shook. "That I would, that I would"

"Well friend what now?" Pelle Rabbit asked

"I am a little hungry and could use a snack... yes yes a snack will do."

"Well since you do not care for rabbit how about some cloud berries?"

"Oh, oh I do love berries."

"Good I know where to find a nice patch."

Kalle Rabbit and Pelle Fox went off together to eat cloud berries and soon became great friends.

About the Author

Stefan Ellery lives in the Kawarthas where he imagines new tales he can bring to life. Many of these tales involve Kalle rabbit and Pelle Fox who are close to his heart. However these two furry friends don't take up all his time, occasionally they let him write other children's stories and novels for young adults.

www.ingramcontent.com/pod-product-compliance
Lightning Source LLC
Chambersburg PA
CBHW041603120626
46551CB00002B/290